Max and Molly's
Guide To Trouble:

How To
Build An
Abominable
Snowman

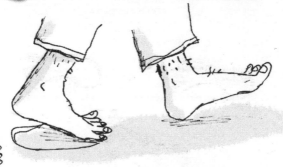

DOMINIC BARKER

ILLUSTRATED BY HANNAH SHAW

ORCHARD

To Daniel Thomas
D.B.

For Tom and Emma
H.S.

ORCHARD BOOKS
338 Euston Road, London NW1 3BH
Orchard Books Australia
Hachette Children's Books
Level 17/207 Kent Street, Sydney, NSW 2000

First published in 2012 by Orchard Books

ISBN 978 1 40830 521 8

Text © Dominic Barker 2012
Illustrations © Hannah Shaw 2012

The rights of Dominic Barker to be identified as the author and
Hannah Shaw to be identified as the illustrator of this work have been asserted
by them in accordance with the Copyright, Designs and Patents Act, 1988.

A CIP catalogue record for this book is available from the British Library.

1 3 5 7 9 10 8 6 4 2

Printed in the UK

Orchard Books is a division of Hachette Children's Books,
an Hachette UK company.

www.hachette.co.uk

A CELLAR FULL OF BEANS

It had been snowing for days in the town of Trull. Snow lay heavy on the trees. Snow lay heavy on the roofs. And, in the back garden of a house on Laburnum Avenue, snow lay heavy on Max Pesker's head.

"Put some more on, Molly!" said Max.

"I'm going as fast as I can, Max," said his twin sister Molly, bending down to scoop up more snow. "But accurate snow-piling is a **VERY DIFFICULT SKILL.**"

Molly had curly red hair and was wearing a blue duffel coat. She climbed onto the chair they had brought out from the dining room and carefully piled more snow on Max's head.

The chair was necessary because Max

had been born twelve minutes before

Molly. According to Max, he had done

a lot of growing in those twelve minutes
and was therefore taller. He had red hair
too, though his was straight, and he was
also wearing a duffel coat. His was pink.
This was because both coats were presents
from their aunt who was violently opposed
to gender stereotyping.

However, Max's pink coat was not the first thing somebody walking into the garden would notice about him. First, they would notice the enormous pyramid of snow on his head. But so far nobody had noticed because Dad was out and Mum was in the kitchen listening to *Radio Trull* and trying to work out how to clean a red wine stain off a gorilla suit. She and Dad had been to a fancy-dress party the night before and Dad had turned out to be a very clumsy King Kong. But all Mum's thoughts of red wine and gorillas disappeared when she looked out of the kitchen window.

First she noticed Max.

Next she noticed Molly.

Then she noticed her best dining-room chair!

Max and Molly heard a violent tapping behind them.

"Don't turn round, Max," said Molly. "The snow pile is the tallest it's ever been."

Max almost nodded but then remembered not to. "What's that noise?" he asked.

Molly looked back at the house.

"It's Mum," she said. "She's tapping on the kitchen window."

"She's probably bored," said Max sympathetically.

"Now she's pointing," commented Molly.

"She's probably pointing at the pile of snow on my head," said Max. "It is very impressive."

"Hmm," said Molly doubtfully.
"Now she's shaking her fist. At least, I think she's shaking her fist. But it's under Dad's gorilla suit, so I'm not completely sure."

"She's probably bored *and* jealous," said Max. "Perhaps she tried to put a big pile of snow on her head when she was younger but it kept sliding off."

"She has got quite a POINTY head," said Molly.

"Not as POINTY as Grandad's," said Max.

"Yes, but remember, Max," said Molly. "We both agreed Grandad is an alien. So his head doesn't count."

The back door opened. "What do you think you're doing with my best new chair?" demanded Mum, waving the gorilla suit at them angrily.

Molly shook her head sadly at her mother. It seemed perfectly obvious what she was doing with the chair.

"I'm standing on it."

"Why are you standing on it?"

"Because otherwise I couldn't reach to put the snow on Max's head," said Molly patiently.

"You are standing on it in your wellies," said Mum icily. "And they are covered in dirty snow."

"You wouldn't want me to be outside in my bare feet," said Molly. "I might get **Frostbite**."

"You'll get a lot more than **Frostbite** if you don't get off the chair this instant."

"But, Mum," protested Max. "Remember that snow is just frozen water."

"I know perfectly well what snow is," replied Mum.

"Well, when it melts it will be like we're washing the chair," said Max.

"Yes," said Molly. "Really you should be thanking us."

"GET. OFF. THE. CHAIR. NOW," said Mum.

Molly and Max knew that when their mum talked in capitals, things had got **SERIOUS**. Reluctantly, Molly climbed down.

"It was nearly ready, too," Molly said.

"What was nearly ready?" demanded Mum.

"The world's first ski jump for guinea pigs. We're building it on Max's head."

"Guinea pigs?"

"We think hamsters could use it too," said Max.

"And gerbils," added Molly.

"And what would happen," said Mum, forgetting for a moment that as far as she knew guinea pigs were unable to ski, "when the guinea pig reached the end of the slope? It would fall to the ground and hurt itself very badly!"

"We've thought of that," said Max.

"We're not cruel," added Molly. "We invented the world's first guinea-pig parachute yesterday."

Mum's mouth dropped open in surprise.

Behind her, Dad marched into the garden. He was wearing two woolly hats, a head torch, ski goggles, an ultra-thick red coat (**Antarctic Protection Level**) and walking boots with crampons attached. In one hand he carried a compass and in the other a thermos of hot soup. Most people might think this was unnecessarily cautious for a trip to the end of the road, but Dad believed in always being prepared for any and every possible CRISIS. He was wearing his "I have some very **IMPORTANT** news" face.

"I have some very **IMPORTANT** news," he said. "Laburnum Avenue is blocked. We're snowed in!"

"Oh dear," said Mum. "You'd think the Mayor and the council would be better prepared for an emergency like this. I was going to drive to the supermarket today. There's nothing in the fridge."

Dad rubbed his gloved hands together with glee. "It's no use relying on mayors and councils. We'll have to go into Survival Mode," he said. "We could be here for months! We'll survive on the baked beans

I keep in the cellar for emergencies."

Max and Molly groaned. They didn't like **beans**. Especially JUST **beans**.

"Don't groan," said Dad sternly. "We must all pull together in this time of CRISIS."

"It's hardly a CRISIS," said Mum.

"Only because we have a cellar full of emergency **beans**," Dad pointed out smugly.

Max and Molly looked at each other. For them, the cellar full of **beans** *was* the CRISIS.

"And get that snow off your head, Max," added Dad. "Do you want to catch hypothermia?"

"Yes," said Max. "I've never had it before."

Max liked collecting unusual things. Including diseases. So far he'd had six (not including colds) and he was always on the lookout for another one.

Unfortunately for Max's disease collection, the snow had other ideas. It slipped from his head and landed with a sad little plop on the ground.

"Poor guinea pigs," said Molly, as
the opportunity for their pets to try
ski jumping disappeared.

"Don't worry about the guinea pigs," said
Dad. "There's enough **beans** for them too!"

And with that he navigated back to the
house using his compass. This wasn't
strictly necessary, as the house was in clear
sight and less than ten metres away, but
Dad liked to keep his survival skills up
to date.

Mum followed with her snow-covered
new chair.

Max and Molly were left to contemplate the awfulness of a diet consisting of nothing but **beans**.

"We have to get Mum to the supermarket," said Max. "Whatever it takes, Laburnum Avenue must be opened!"

THE MAN WITH NO STORY

In Studio 1 of *Radio Trull*,
it was time for the news. Carl Pilge, the
twenty-five-year-old newsreader and
reporter, cleared his throat as the sound
of the final pip faded.

"This is *Radio Trull* and I'm

Carl Pilge," he announced. "Here are the news headlines. Snow blankets Trull leading to transport chaos. The Mayor is blamed for being unprepared. Latest polls suggest he will lose next week's election unless he can turn things round dramatically. And now over to Kirsty with the traffic..."

Carl Pilge clicked his microphone to OFF AIR. Just then, the boss of *Radio Trull* burst into the studio. Mr Sykes' normal mood was **VERY ANGRY**. But today was obviously special because he looked at Carl with **INTENSE FURY**.

"**Pilge!**" he bellowed, waving a piece of paper in his face. "**Have you seen the latest listener figures?**"

"Er...no," admitted Carl Pilge. "Are they...er...good?"

"**Good?**" Sykes' eyes bulged. "**They are terrible. And do you know who's to blame?**"

"The internet?" suggested Carl.

"**You!**" Sykes told him.

"Me?"

"**You, Pilge! You are a useless reporter. When was the last time you reported a good story?**"

"I couldn't find—" began Carl, but Sykes was in no mood for excuses.

"**Couldn't find a story? We've got snow! We've got the Mayoral election next week! Why, when I was a young reporter I'd have had a story featuring both of them with a tearful-human-interest angle by teatime.**"

"The Mayor. Snow. Tearful Human Interest," said Carl Pilge. "But the day's almost half over—"

"Pilge! Bring me a gripping and dramatic story by teatime or you're fired!" Mr Sykes stomped out of the studio and slammed the door behind him.

Carl Pilge slumped over the newsdesk in despair. *Gripping* and DRAMATIC things never happened in Trull. It was *hopeless*.

things that NEVER

happen in Trull

POET MOLLYET

"We're not getting anywhere," said Max, putting down his spade.

"You're right," agreed Molly, dropping her bucket. "There's almost as much snow as when we started."

The prospect of living off emergency

beans had forced Max and Molly into drastic action. They had decided to dig out a clear route so Mum could drive to the supermarket and buy them something nicer for tea. Like **pizza**. Unfortunately their plan didn't seem to be working.

"We must've been digging for at least two hours by now," said Max.

"More like three," said Molly.

In fact, Max and Molly had been shovelling snow for a little less than ten minutes. But when you're trying to clear

heavy drifts of snow on a blocked road
using only a small toy bucket and spade,
ten minutes can seem like a *very* long time.

"This is useless," decided Max. "We need
a New Plan."

Max and Molly looked around them. They
both firmly believed that if you needed a
New Plan, one was bound to turn up.

Just then, Benedict and Imogen Goodley
came out of the house opposite. Max and
Molly looked at each other and nodded.
Obviously the Goodleys were part of
whatever the New Plan was.

"Come over here!" shouted Max.

"We need a New Plan!" cried Molly.

Benedict and Imogen looked at each
other nervously.

The Goodleys were the best, politest, kindest children in Trull (all the adults said so). They could each play two musical instruments and could say "*Please*" and "*Thank you*" in ten foreign languages. Max and Molly couldn't play anything and thought that saying "*Please*" and "*Thank you*" wasted time that could be spent saying MUCH MORE IMPORTANT THINGS.

**things to say
which are important**

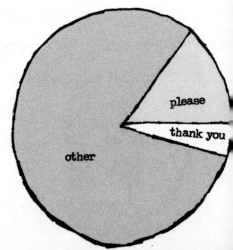

please

thank you

other

The Goodleys were well aware that talking to Max and Molly normally led to trouble. And if there was one thing the Goodley children hated more than anything else, it was getting into trouble. But they were also very well brought up children who knew that when someone asked you for help you should try your best to assist them. Reluctantly, they walked over to Max and Molly.

Max noticed that Imogen and Benedict were both carrying notebooks. "What are they for?" he wanted to know.

"Writing down New Plans?" Molly suggested hopefully.

"Er...not really," said Benedict.

"They are for writing POEMS," explained Imogen.

"POEMS?" said Max. "Why are you writing POEMS?"

"Daddy said that we should," said Benedict.

"He felt that the snow might inspire us," said Imogen.

"Why would it do that?" asked Molly.

"I'm not really sure," admitted Benedict.

"He said something about *the wonder of the natural world*," Imogen reminded him.

"That was it," remembered Benedict. "*The wonder of the natural world*. He said we should contemplate it."

Max and Molly took a moment to contemplate *the wonder of the natural world*.

"It's just Laburnum Avenue with snow on it," Max said finally.

"Yes," agreed Molly. "So forget about that and help us with something much more **IMPORTANT**."

Benedict and Imogen looked at one another uncomfortably. They knew helping was a good thing. But on the other hand...

"Daddy did say he was looking forward to reading our new poems," said Imogen.

Molly sighed. It was obvious that if she was going to get a plan she would need to provide a poem first.

ax, confused. "Aren't
the roads? Why would
n them?"
merick about road
tition," said Molly.

ung lady called Polly,
front of a lorry,
at,
flat,
be safe and not sorry!"

e stopped to consider the
oem.

"Pass it here," she said holding out
her hand.

Imogen handed over her notebook and
pen. Molly opened it, scribbled something
on the first page and handed it straight
back.

Imogen read what Molly had written
out loud:

Snow snow
You gotta go
Or else it means
We have to eat beans!

Imogen looked at Molly doubtfully.

"It's a poem," said Molly.

"It rhymes," agreed Max.

"I'm not sure there's much about *the wonder of the natural world*," said Benedict, as tactfully as he could.

"It's about the snow," said Molly. "Snow's nature, isn't it?"

"So are beans," added Max supportively. "That's two bits of nature in only one poem. Your dad will love it. Now you've got to help us with our plan."

"What about *my* poem?" said Benedict.

"Bollards?" said M

they the things on

you want to write

"I once wrote a l

safety for a compe

"There was a yo

Who ran out in

She used to be

But now she is

So you should

The other thre

merits of this p

"It didn't win," said Molly sadly.
"But I don't think the judge liked me
because I asked if he was wearing a wig."

CHILDREN
IN NEED

Max and Molly told Benedict and Imogen
about the problem of being snowed in with
only emergency **beans** to eat. Now they
were waiting patiently for them to come
up with a New Plan to solve it.

"Hurry up!" said Molly, who really wasn't

that good at waiting patiently. "Each second without a plan brings us ever closer to our first plate of **beans**!"

Benedict and Imogen weren't exactly sure how they had become responsible for coming up with a New Plan, but they decided to make the best of it.

"What exactly do you want?" asked Benedict.

"We want to unblock the road so we don't have to eat emergency **beans** for tea."

"You could come to our house for tea,"

Imogen offered generously. "We're having **TOFU**."

"Is that like **toffee**?" said Molly.

"Er..." Benedict and Imogen both looked embarrassed.

"We don't know," admitted Benedict.

"It's not a hard question," scoffed Molly. "It either is or it isn't."

"The thing is," explained Benedict, "we've never actually eaten **toffee**."

Max and Molly were **flabbergasted**. "Never eaten **toffee**!"

"Mum says that it's bad for our teeth," said Imogen.

"We've never had any sweets," said Benedict.

"Or any sugary drinks," added Imogen.

"Or any ice cream," finished Benedict.

Max and Molly were **double flabbergasted**. No sweets! No sugary drinks! No ice cream! They looked at each other solemnly.

"Molly," said Max. "It just goes to show that there are always people worse off than us."

"Yes, Max," agreed Molly. "Here's us worrying about **beans**, while the poor Goodleys have never even tasted a sweet."

"I'm not sure we're worse off than you," said Benedict. "It's just that our parents believe—"

"Nonsense," interrupted Molly. "You are CHILDREN IN NEED."

"IN NEED?" said Imogen.

"IN NEED of sweets," said Molly.

Max felt the situation was so serious that he should make the Goodleys

feel better. And whenever he wanted anyone to feel better he told them a gruesome fact about the natural world.

"Did you know that a **bullet ant** causes the most painful sting in the world? According to the **Schmidt Pain Index** it's like walking over flaming charcoal with a three-inch rusty nail in your heel."

Max watched as the Goodleys digested this information. It didn't seem to make them feel better.

The snow began falling once more. Molly decided to focus matters back to the task in hand. "This makes it even more important that we clear the road. Not only do we have to save me and Max from **beans**, we also have to get you some **toffee**!"

"A snowplough," said Benedict suddenly. "That's how you open roads again."

"Where are we going to get one of those?" Max wanted to know.

"I think the council have them," Benedict said.

"OK, that sounds easy," said Molly. "We'll just ring them up and ask them to send one round."

"I'm not sure," said Benedict. "I think they normally clear the main roads first."

"But that's because they don't know about our beans and toffee emergency," said Molly. "Once they hear about it, they'll send a snowplough round immediately."

"Hmm," said Benedict doubtfully.

But Molly was already marching off towards her house.

SNOW CHANCE

Betty Buttons operated the telephone
switchboard at Trull Council. Due to
the bad weather she had been answering
five times more calls than usual, and
was perhaps a little stressed. However,
she was dedicated to her job, and despite

the difficulties of the day she answered
the phone with her normal cheery
politeness.

"Good afternoon! You've reached Trull
Council. My name is Betty Buttons. How
may I help you?"

"Hello," said the voice on the other
end. "I'd like you to send a snowplough to
Laburnum Avenue immediately, please!"

The voice sounded **suspiciously** young
to be ordering a snowplough.

"Thank you for calling the council," said Betty politely. "Could I ask you for your name and to repeat your request, please?"

"My name is Molly Pesker. I live in Laburnum Avenue and I need a snow plough immediately."

"I'm afraid all our snowploughs are busy dealing with the current unexpected snow fall."

"Not in Laburnum Avenue, they're not."

Betty Buttons punched a few keys on her computer. A map of the local area appeared. Some it was red. Some of it was

orange. Some of it was yellow and some of
it was green.

"I'm afraid that Laburnum Avenue has
been designated a green low-priority area
according to the council's most recent
Snow Response Plan."

"What does that mean?"

"It means that the council will only direct a snowplough to deal with the snow after it has removed the snow in the red, orange and yellow areas."

"When will that be?"

Betty punched a couple more keys.

"According to my computer this will be in approximately two weeks' time."

"Two weeks! But I might be dead by then."

Betty was alarmed. "Dead? Why?"

"Beans!"

"**beans?**"

"My dad says we've got to eat emergency **beans** until the snow's cleared."

"Poisonous emergency **beans**?" asked Betty Buttons.

"No," admitted Molly. "Normal **beans**. But after two weeks I might be dead anyway. They always say at school that if you don't have a balanced diet it can be dangerous for your health in the long run. And two weeks sounds like a long run to me. Because if I had to run for two weeks I'd be exhausted."

Betty Buttons' temper began to fray around the edges.

"Young lady. You will not be killed by two weeks of **baked beans**. Now I must ask you to hang up. There are people trying to contact the council with serious problems, not to mention that we are very busy because of next week's Mayoral elections."

There was a slight pause at the other end of the phone while Molly took in the news that the council were not going to send a snowplough in order to save her from a diet of **beans**. She decided she would have to use her even more serious information.

"There are also two children here who've never tasted **toffee**," she informed Betty.

"**Toffee! beans!**" cried Betty Buttons,

whose temper was no longer frayed but well and truly torn. "I have other callers. I'm afraid I must end this call."

And she abruptly ended the call.

"That was very rude," observed Molly. She went back outside to inform the others of the council's incredible decision not to divert a snowplough to Laburnum Avenue, despite knowing the TRUE HORROR that she, Max, Imogen and Benedict were facing.

Max could see the disappointment etched on his sister's face, and being a sensitive brother he immediately acted to make her feel better.

"The tarantula hawk is really a type of spider wasp. Its sting causes pain which is normally described as blinding, fierce and shockingly electric," he told her.

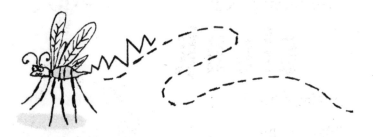

Amazingly, this gruesome fact failed to make Molly feel better.

"It's not fair," said Molly. "Just because we're children the council thinks it can ignore us."

"Yes," agreed Max.

"I should have said that on the phone to Betty," said Molly.

Something went

clunk

in Max's head.

"Betty!" he said.

"That's it!"

"What about Betty?" Molly asked.

"Not Betty," said Max, beside himself with excitement. "But rhyming her name gave me the answer."

"My dad says poetry will save the world," remarked Benedict.

"What's the answer?" demanded Molly.

"Yeti!"

LAYERS UPON HIMALAYAS

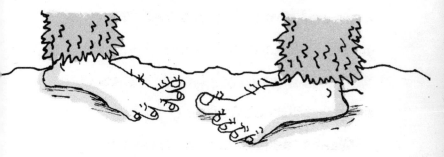

"Yeti! Bigfoot! THE ABOMINABLE SNOWMAN!"

"Have you gone mad, Max?" asked Molly.

Max shook his head. "Think what the Mayor and the council would do if it knew THE ABOMINABLE SNOWMAN was loose in Laburnum Avenue."

Molly, Benedict and Imogen all looked at Max with blank faces. They had no idea what the Mayor and the council would do if it discovered there was an ABOMINABLE SNOWMAN loose in Laburnum Avenue.

Max couldn't believe they were all being so stupid. "They'd have to clear the snow!" he told them. "To make THE ABOMINABLE SNOWMAN lose his natural habitat so he'd have to go back to the Himalayas."

"He could become the THE ABOMINABLE PAVEMENT MAN instead," Molly pointed out.

"You can't be ABOMINABLE on a pavement," insisted Max. "They're too boring."

Molly considered pavements for a moment. Max was right. They were quite boring. "Shall I go and phone Betty Buttons at the council and tell them about THE ABOMINABLE SNOWMAN?"

"Er..." said Benedict awkwardly. "Don't you think that she might not believe you?"

Molly considered this possibility. "Why?" she said.

"Well, like Max said. Normally THE ABOMINABLE SNOWMAN lives in the Himalayas. The council might want to know why he's suddenly moved to Trull."

"Oh! Sorry," said Max.

"I think if we call the council and ask them to send round a snowplough because we've seen THE ABOMINABLE SNOWMAN, they would say no," said Benedict.

The others reflected on Benedict's view and reluctantly concluded he was probably right.

"Adults can be pesky," said Molly. "They never just believe you."

"But to be fair," said Imogen, "we aren't telling the truth."

Molly gave a Imogen a hard stare.
"It's very rude to call somebody a liar,"
she said.

Without quite knowing how, Imogen
felt she was in the wrong. "I'm sorry,"
she said. "I didn't mean to be rude."

"That's all right," said Molly generously.

"We'll have to get the adults to believe us," said Max.

"My dad says most people believe anything they're told by the media," said Benedict.

"The media?" said Molly. "Who are they?"

"The people on the television and the radio," said Benedict. "If they say something is true then people believe them."

"Wow!" said Max. "So if I got someone on the radio to say that we should have more **VENOMOUS** things in Trull then the council would just go and get them?"

"Well, I'm not—"

"We could have **BLACK WIDOWS** and *vipers* and BOX JELLYFISH—"

"BOX JELLYFISH?" said Molly who, being Max's sister, knew that BOX JELLYFISH were the most **VENOMOUS** creatures on the planet. "Where would we put BOX JELLYFISH?"

"In the swimming pool," answered Max impatiently.

"But wouldn't they kill all the swimmers?"

Max reflected on this problem for a moment and found a brilliant solution.

"They would have their own lane," he announced. "There would be a slow lane, a medium lane, and a BOX JELLYFISH lane!"

"You'd swim really fast in that lane," said Molly.

"What have BOX JELLYFISH got to do with THE ABOMINABLE SNOWMAN?" asked Imogen, completely confused.

Molly realised they had absolutely nothing to do with it. And teatime was getting closer. And that meant beans! "I'm going to ring Radio Trull," she said. "And tell them about the Yeti."

"No!" said Benedict. "First we need some evidence. They won't believe the story unless there's some kind of evidence."

"What kind of evidence?" said Molly.

Benedict didn't know.

"Benedict," said Molly crossly. "It isn't helpful to invent problems you don't know how to solve."

But Max had an idea. "What's THE ABOMINABLE SNOWMAN's other name?"

"The **Yeti**!" said Imogen.

Max shook his head. "His other other name."

The others had forgotten.

"**Bigfoot!**" Max reminded them. "So what we need are some really **big** footprints."

"Who's got the **biggest** feet in the street?" said Molly.

Max remembered the feet of their next-door neighbour. "Jeremy! If we can get him to make some footprints in the snow, they'll be the evidence the radio people need."

"Why would he go walking out in the snow in bare feet?" wondered Imogen.

The children were silent for a moment. Walking in the snow in bare feet was not the sort of thing that it was easy to persuade adults to do.

"I've got an idea," said Molly suddenly. "It said on the TV this morning that you should visit your elderly neighbours in the bad weather to see if they are all right and not **AT RISK**."

"I don't understand how seeing if Jeremy is all right will get him walking barefoot in the snow," said Max.

"What if he had to prove he was all right and not **AT RISK** by passing a test?" said Molly. "We could make him do it."

Benedict was horrified.

"We're children," he protested. "We're not allowed to tell adults what to do. They're supposed to tell us what to do."

Max and Molly looked at him as though he was crazy.

"We tell adults what to do all the time," Max assured him.

"It's for their own good," explained Molly. "Without our help they wouldn't be any use at all."

Benedict and Imogen Goodley exchanged horrified glances. But Max and Molly were already walking towards Jeremy's house. The Goodleys had said they would help. It was too late to back out now.

SCARE IN THE COMMUNITY

The doorbell rang long and loud at number eight Laburnum Avenue.

"Coming!" shouted Jeremy, clicking 'Save' on his laptop.

Jeremy had recently moved into Laburnum Avenue. He was a very tall, skinny man who worked from home on his computer. He opened the door. Max and Molly Pesker, and Benedict and Imogen Goodley were standing there. Which was strange. What was stranger was that none of them were looking up at him. They were all looking down.

"They are really **big**," Jeremy thought he heard one of the children say.

"What was that?" said Jeremy, already a little worried. Jeremy was one of those nervous adults who were scared of children.

They all looked up at once. "Nothing," they chorused.

"What do...er...that is to say...what do you want?" asked Jeremy.

Jeremy was especially nervous because two of the children were Max and Molly. You didn't need to live in Laburnum Avenue for long to come across them.

They were exactly the kind of children who scared him the most. But at the same time Jeremy was comforted by the sight of Benedict and Imogen – the two most well-behaved children in the whole of Trull. Always quiet and polite. You almost wouldn't know they were there. If only all children could be like them.

"We've come to see if you're all right," announced Molly sweetly.

"All right?" said Jeremy puzzled. "Apart from the fact that I have a project deadline today and the internet is down because of the snow and the Mayor isn't doing anything about it. Apart from that, I'm fine. Why wouldn't I be?"

"They said on the TV," explained Max, "that in this time of bad weather we should visit the elderly to see if they're OK."

"I'm twenty-eight," said Jeremy, a little offended. "That's not elderly."

"It is," Molly assured him confidently. "You are **AT RISK**!"

Jeremy was a bit taken aback by Molly's certainty. "What kind of **RISK**?" he asked.

"**RISKY RISK**," said Molly.

"That's the worst kind," Max told him.

"But what does that mean?" persisted Jeremy.

"We won't know that until we've fully evaluated your situation," said Molly. "But it could be very **RISKY**."

"As **RISKY** as accidentally disturbing a hive of killer bees in Mexico," emphasised Max.

"I don't want to..." began Jeremy but then he noticed the pleading eyes of Benedict and Imogen Goodley and realised what was happening (or at least what he thought was happening). Could it be, he wondered, that these good children had decided to reform Max and Molly, to use their influence to turn the WORST behaved children in the street into the best behaved children? It would be wrong not to help them.

"All right," agreed Jeremy. "If you would like to help me then it would be rude to refuse your kind offer."

"Very rude," added Molly.

"So what would you like me to do?"

"We'd like you to come outside, please."

"But I thought I was **AT RISK**," said Jeremy. "Surely I should stay inside and keep warm?"

All four children shook their heads.

"I shouldn't stay inside and keep warm?" he repeated.

"Absolutely not," said Max.

"That would be the **VERY WORST** thing," said Molly.

"Well, not absolutely the WORST—"
began Benedict, but Molly interrupted him.

"The **VERY WORST** thing."

"Why?" said Jeremy.

"You need to stimulate your body,"
said Molly. "If you place it in a cold
environment then it will respond by
working harder to warm you up. Then
when you go back inside you will no
longer be **AT RISK**."

"Couldn't I just turn the central heating
up?" asked Jeremy.

The four children shook their heads.

"What if there was a POWER CUT?"
said Max.

"We don't usually have POWER CUTS,"
said Jeremy. "I can't remember the last one.
I mean…"

"You would be **AT RISK**," Max
informed Jeremy solemnly.

Jeremy still wasn't exactly sure *what*
RISK he was at but before he could
try and find out more Max added,
"It's the latest **scientific** advice."

And," added Molly firmly, "nobody can
argue with **science**."

Jeremy really didn't want to leave his warm house and go out into the cold snow. But he looked again at the pleading eyes of the Goodleys. However strange, it seemed they truly wanted to help him. Perhaps this was the time to try and conquer his fear of children.

"Let me just put on my coat and my wellies," he said.

"There's no need—" began Imogen, but Max and Molly SHUSHED her.

Jeremy put on his coat and wellies and

followed the children outside. The snow
had stopped. But it was still piled high in
the street.

"First," said Molly. "We need to take the
temperature of your nose."

"My nose?" said Jeremy, already
beginning to regret coming out.

"It's science," Molly informed him.
She pulled a thermometer out of her
pocket. "Place this in your nose."

"Is this really necessary?" asked Jeremy.

"In your nose," Molly insisted. "And try
not to sneeze."

Reluctantly, Jeremy placed the
thermometer in his nose.

"Now, give it back please," said Molly.

"But it hasn't had
time to take a
reading yet,"
said Jeremy.

"I hope you are not arguing with **science**, Jeremy," said Molly sternly.

Jeremy's fear of children wasn't going away. If anything, it was getting worse. Meekly, he handed the thermometer to Molly. She studied it and then passed it to Max who shook his head and gave it to Benedict who said "TSSK" and gave it to Imogen who looked sadly at the result.

Jeremy was alarmed by these reactions. "What's the matter?" he wanted to know.

"You have a very **lazy** body," Molly informed him.

"Do I?" said Jeremy.

"This calls for drastic measures," Max said. "We have to create a situation which forces your **lazy** body into action."

"But I'm not that **lazy**," protested Jeremy. "I play squash on Tuesdays."

"Remove your wellies and your socks!" ordered Molly.

"What?" cried Jeremy. "Why?"

"Because," explained Max, "when your bare feet walk through the cold snow your body will be stimulated to heat you up."

"A nice cup of tea would do that, wouldn't it?" said Jeremy desperately.

The four children shook their heads.

"I really have to take them off?" said Jeremy.

The four children nodded.

"Imogen will hold them," Molly informed him.

"Will I?" said Imogen.

Reluctantly Jeremy removed his wellies and his socks and handed them to Imogen, who held them as far away as possible from her face.

"Now if you could just walk through the snow for about twenty paces towards our house," said Max, "your body should start to warm you up."

"Why does it have to be in the direction of your house?" asked Jeremy, fearing that he already knew the answer.

"Science," confirmed Molly.

Jeremy wasn't quite sure how he'd ended up here. All he knew was that he had four expectant faces looking up at him.

He took a few steps in the snow. "IT'S COLD," he said.

"That's a good sign," said Max.

"Your feet are responding well."

"Good feet," added Molly approvingly.

Jeremy felt that if his feet were responding well they would be running as fast as they could back to his house and getting into a warm bath.

"Just a few more steps," said Max encouragingly.

"Towards our house," Molly reminded him.

"Then I can definitely go?" said Jeremy.

Max, Molly, Benedict and Imogen nodded.

Jeremy walked as fast as he could towards Max and Molly's house.

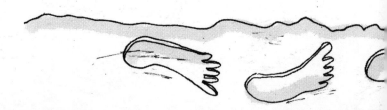

"Remember to press as hard as you can," called Max. "The depth of the footprint is very important."

Jeremy stopped. "My feet are turning blue," he cried.

"That is a **FANTASTIC** sign," commented Max. "They have responded well to the challenge and your level of **RISK** can now be measured accurately."

"What is it?"

"No **RISK**," said Max.

"You may go home," confirmed Molly.

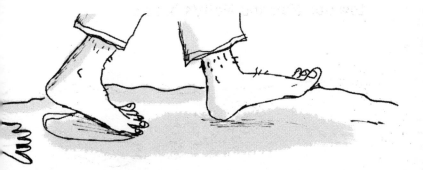

"Would you like to know about your chances of surviving an attack from a **Great White Shark** first?" asked Max.

It turned out Jeremy wouldn't. Gathering his wellies and his socks, he rushed back to the safety of his home and resolved not to open his door again until the snow had melted.

Max and Molly gave each other a nod of satisfaction. Jeremy's footprints were enough evidence to convince the media that THE ABOMINABLE SNOWMAN was on the loose and that they needed to clear the snow and send him packing again.

The plan to get Mum to the supermarket was working perfectly!

FANCY THAT!

"Hello. This is *Radio Trull*. Daisy Fountain speaking," said Daisy Fountain.

"I'd like to speak to somebody about THE ABOMINABLE SNOWMAN, please," said Molly.

"I beg your pardon?"

"THE ABOMINABLE SNOWMAN."

"Er..." Daisy Fountain paused. She knew who was responsible for music and who was responsible for sport and who was responsible for news. She decided THE ABOMINABLE SNOWMAN came under news.

"Putting you through now, caller."

The phone rang on Carl Pilge's desk. Carl wasted no time in picking it up. He'd only got two hours left to save his job and so far he hadn't had a sniff of a **gripping** and DRAMATIC story.

"Hello," he said. "Carl Pilge. *Radio Trull* newsdesk."

"THE ABOMINABLE SNOWMAN is loose in Laburnum Avenue."

"What?"

"THE ABOMINABLE SNOWMAN. You've got to tell people. He's travelled here from the Himalayas because Trull has got nicer local amenities and is close to many major transport hubs."

Carl was lost for words. This was undoubtedly the strangest story anybody had ever reported to him.

"Are you going to put it on the radio?"

"Er...well. I'll need evidence," said Carl.

"There's evidence," insisted the voice.

"Really?" Carl was surprised. "Like a sighting?"

"Well...not exactly. But there are footprints."

"Footprints?"

"Big footprints!"

"I can't put a report on the radio based on just footprints."

"Can't you?"

"NO!"

There was a brief pause on the other end of the line. "There was a sighting as well!"

"Really?"

"Yes! I forgot!"

"You *forgot* a sighting of THE ABOMINABLE SNOWMAN?"

"Yes! But now I've remembered. So could you put it in the news...?"

"NO," said Carl firmly. "I'll have to see it myself."

"Really? You couldn't just take my word for it?"

"NO."

"Well, I suppose so. But hurry up. It's not that long till teatime."

"What's teatime got to do with anything?"

"Nothing... Just come to Laburnum Avenue right away."

The phone went dead.

Carl Pilge thought for a moment. This was obviously a joke. THE ABOMINABLE SNOWMAN in Trull. It was nonsense. But then he remembered that if he wanted to save his job then he had to find a good story.

Knowing that things couldn't possibly get any worse, he pulled on his coat, walked out of the headquarters of *Radio Trull*, and began the cold trudge to Laburnum Avenue.

Meanwhile, Max, Benedict and Imogen were looking expectantly at Molly.

"He wants to see THE ABOMINABLE SNOWMAN if he's going to put it on the radio."

"See it?" said Benedict

"But THE ABOMINABLE SNOWMAN isn't here," pointed out Imogen. "He can't see him."

"We just have to accept that we have failed," admitted Benedict. "I will go back to writing my poem."

"FAILED?" said Max and Molly

scornfully. "Of course we haven't failed."

"But he said he wanted to see THE ABOMINABLE SNOWMAN."

"Well then," said Max. "We'll have to show him."

"But how…"

Suddenly Molly remembered what Mum had been holding that morning.

Dad's gorilla outfit!

TRACKING IT DOWN

Carl Pilge was not in a good mood by the time he arrived in Laburnum Avenue.

His shoes had leaked and his feet were wet.

He couldn't believe he had walked more than a mile in the freezing cold for an alleged sighting of THE ABOMINABLE SNOWMAN.

If he didn't find a story then he was going to lose his job. But at least he'd have lost his job with dry feet.

A small girl ran up to him the moment he arrived in the street.

"I'm Molly Pesker," she said. "Are you the reporter from *Radio Trull*?"

Carl nodded miserably. He'd known the voice on the phone sounded a bit young, but this was ridiculous. *Maybe I deserve to lose my job*, thought Carl glumly. *After all, if I'm stupid enough to come all this way in the cold because a little girl said she'd seen*

THE ABOMINABLE SNOWMAN *then I'm*
probably not cut out to be a reporter.

"Hurry up!" said Molly.

"Maybe this isn't such a good idea,"
said Carl.

"Of course it isn't a good idea," replied
Molly sternly. "THE ABOMINABLE
SNOWMAN in Laburnum Avenue is a
terrible idea. He might eat us. Come and
look at these footprints."

And she marched off to show him.

"But…" Carl realised his life couldn't get much worse. When he'd made the decision to be a reporter he had imagined himself asking hard questions and exposing big stories. It hadn't quite worked out that way. And now…now he was being bossed about by a little girl.

"Come on," ordered Molly fiercely.

Carl Pilge walked a little further up the street.

"Look!" Molly pointed at the marks in the snow.

Carl looked down to see some big footprints. "Those are big footprints," he observed.

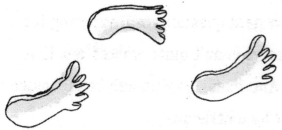

"Exactly," said Molly. "They are the footprints of THE ABOMINABLE SNOWMAN!"

Carl Pilge, however, had another explanation. "They could just be the footprints of a man with BIG FEET."

Molly was a little surprised by this response. "Of course they're not!"

"That's what they look like to me," said Carl Pilge.

"Have you ever seen a **Yeti's** footprints?" demanded Molly.

"No," admitted Carl Pilge.

"Then how do you know that these aren't them?"

"Because they look more like the prints of a man with bare feet to me."

"But why would he be out in bare feet?" said Molly a little desperately. "If he was a man then he'd be wearing wellies. Only a **Yeti** would be out in bare feet in this weather."

Carl Pilge shrugged. "Sometimes people do strange things," he said.

Molly gave Carl Pilge a hard stare. "I don't think you're a very good reporter," she said.

"That's what my boss thinks," agreed Carl Pilge glumly.

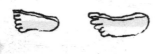

"If you were a good reporter you would say: *Perhaps we should follow the tracks. They might lead us to a brief glimpse of* THE ABOMINABLE SNOWMAN."

Carl Pilge was discovering that his day could get worse. But sometimes when people are having really bad days they just keep going to see how much worse it will get.

"Let's follow the tracks then," Carl sighed.

HEADING FOR DISASTER

"It's getting really hot in here," said
Benedict. "And you're heavier than
I thought."

Max sympathised with Benedict's
complaint. They were both squeezed inside
the gorilla outfit which was just

a bit too small for two boys. Max was sitting on Benedict's shoulders. He decided to make Benedict feel a little better.

"It's winter," he told him, "so your chances of being attacked by a GRIZZLY BEAR are low because they should be hibernating."

Inside the suit, Benedict showed no signs of feeling any better.

"I wish I'd just written poetry instead," said Imogen, who was standing next to them.

Max was still holding the head of the gorilla outfit. He didn't want to put it on until the last possible moment. Balancing precariously on Benedict's shoulders, he took a quick peek round the corner of his house.

"The reporter's here!" he told Benedict.

Underneath him, Benedict was beginning to have SECOND THOUGHTS.

"We haven't practised walking properly," he muttered.

"It doesn't matter," said Max. "All the reporter needs is one tiny glimpse of

THE ABOMINABLE SNOWMAN. One or two steps where he can see us, then back behind here to take the costume off. We'll be fine."

"One or two steps," repeated Benedict doubtfully. "I don't know if..."

"Too late," said Max. "They're coming! Get ready, Imogen!"

Max popped the gorilla head on. THE ABOMINABLE SNOWMAN was about to make its first appearance in Trull.

Molly was leading Carl Pilge towards the house following the trail of big footprints, when suddenly there was a SCREAM.

Carl Pilge looked up to see another small girl running out from behind the corner of one of the houses. For the first time since he arrived in Laburnum Avenue he began to wonder... Could it be...?

The girl SCREAMED again as she ran towards them.

"What's the matter?" asked Molly.

"The...the...the..." said the other girl, pointing desperately behind her.

"What can it be?" said Molly.

"Ab... Ab... Ab..."

"She can hardly talk because she's so terrified," Molly told Carl Pilge.

"ABOMINABLE SNOWMAN!"

"*No!*" cried Molly.

"Yes!" screeched Imogen. "Look!"

Carl Pilge looked.

And there it was.

THE ABOMINABLE SNOWMAN.

In Trull.

The **Yeti** had emerged from just behind Max and Molly's house. It was dark, and it was hairy. It looked towards them and beat its chest with its furry brown arms.

Imogen screamed again.

The **Yeti** waved at them.

"I think this is an AGGRESSIVE DISPLAY," Molly informed Carl Pilge. "It could feel we're threatening its territory. You can write that down if you like so you don't forget it in your report."

Carl Pilge said nothing. He was continuing to stare at the **Yeti**.

Imogen SCREAMED again.

"Imogen's SCREAMING," Molly commented.

"I know," said Carl Pilge, whose ears were already ringing.

"We'll probably only get one glimpse

of the **Yeti**," Molly said, sounding amazingly calm for somebody who was looking at a terrifying beast. "I think ABOMINABLE SNOWMEN are quite shy really. He'll probably be off in a minute."

As if on cue, THE ABOMINABLE SNOWMAN turned back in the direction it had come from. However, it appeared to be having trouble moving, and for a while remained stubbornly rooted to the spot. Eventually, with some difficulty, it moved one leg. This seemed to unbalance it and it began to sway.

Then it waved its arms wildly in an attempt to steady itself. Then it fell over backwards and landed with a plop in the snow. Then its head fell off.

Carl Pilge saw that THE ABOMINABLE SNOWMAN was, in fact, Max and Benedict.

Molly tried desperately to improvise.

"My twin brother is a **Yeti**!" she cried.

Carl Pilge gave her a hard stare. Molly realised it hadn't worked.

"Looks like it's emergency **beans** for tea," she said sadly.

"What?" said Carl Pilge.

"**beans** for tea," explained Molly. "Today, tomorrow. Maybe forever."

Carl Pilge's reporter's brain decided to ask one last question.

"Why?"

PLOUGHING ON!

Mum was in the kitchen doing some washing. The radio was on but she wasn't really listening. And then suddenly something caught her attention...

"We go over live now to Laburnum Avenue where *Radio Trull*'s own

Carl Pilge has an exclusive story about how the continued snowfall is bringing real **HARDSHIP** to some of Trull's youngest residents..."

Mum took a deep breath and hoped it had nothing to do with...

"Max and Molly Pesker. Two young children who are going to have to suffer more than most in the next few days. I'm Carl Pilge and I'm here **LIVE** with them and their friends, Benedict and Imogen. Max, Molly, tell our listeners what you're forced to eat because of the snow blocking your road."

"Emergency **beans**," said Molly.

"COLD emergency **beans**?" said the reporter.

"They could be cold," Mum heard Molly agree. "And they're from the cellar."

"And I bet that cellar is really dark and dirty and nasty, isn't it?" said Carl Pilge.

"Yes," said Molly.

"It's so dark," added Max, "that there could be a **VENOMOUS** spider in there and you'd never know until it bit you."

"Now, you rang the Mayor and the council to tell them about this, and what did they say?" continued Carl Pilge.

"They said we've got to eat the **beans**," said Molly. "They didn't care."

"Is this making you cry?" asked Carl, remembering his boss's orders.

"I'm certainly sniffing," said Molly. "But I could be getting a cold."

"So there we have it, listeners," Carl Pilge summed up, "two WEEPING children condemned to eat cold emergency **beans** from a cellar potentially filled with

VENOMOUS spiders in our own home town of Trull. What a terrible indictment on our whole society! Will nobody think of the children? And now, back to the studio."

Mum had heard enough. She ran out of the kitchen, banging into Dad on the way.

"Did Max and Molly just **INSULT** my cellar on the radio?" he said.

Mum put on her wellies and grabbed her coat.

"I'm very proud of that cellar," said Dad forlornly.

"Oh dear," said Molly, seeing Mum come tearing down the drive. "I was hoping her radio wasn't on."

The Goodleys were not used to the sight of angry adults. "I think we should be getting on with our poems, Imogen," said Benedict.

Imogen nodded. The Goodleys hurried off home. Mum was still heading directly for Max and Molly.

"Do you think if I told her that there is one crocodile in Africa that has grown so big it once ate a **WHOLE HIPPOPOTAMUS**, it would help?" wondered Max.

Molly didn't think so.

Mum stormed over to them. "What are you two up to?" she demanded. "I don't want everyone thinking I'm giving you cold **beans** for tea!"

"Well, I never actually said they were cold," said Molly.

"And your father is very upset about people thinking his cellar is dirty. You two are going to come back inside and go right up to your bedrooms where you will stay for the rest of the—"

Suddenly Mum stopped shouting. A vehicle was roaring into Laburnum Avenue. Max and Molly turned round.

A snowplough!

It powered up the street, clearing away the snow as it did so, and came to an abrupt halt beside Max and Molly.

A man with a gold chain around his neck jumped out.

"The **MAYOR!**" said Mum.

"Where's that reporter?" said the Mayor.

"Here!" said Carl Pilge.

"Can you put me on the radio, young man?"

Carl Pilge grinned. His story was getting better by the minute. He called the station and demanded they put him on air straightaway. This was an exclusive.

He held his microphone out to the Mayor.

"I just want to say to your listeners," said the Mayor, "that when I heard about the TERRIBLE plight of Max and Molly Pesker on *Radio Trull* I immediately hopped on a snowplough to come and rescue them from cold emergency **beans** and VENOMOUS spiders."

"But—" began Mum, but the Mayor carried on.

"Let me reassure the citizens of Trull that their Mayor will never let children suffer, whatever the weather."

"They weren't suff—" Mum tried again.

"Children and families are my top priority and I want every voter – I mean citizen – to remember that in next week's election. When you go to vote, think of Max and Molly. Thank you."

"And now, back to the studio," said Carl Pilge.

The radio broadcast was over.

The Mayor shook Max and Molly's hands, then leapt back on the snowplough and drove off, leaving a clear street behind him.

Carl Pilge's phone rang. He picked
it up.

"That's what I meant, Pilge," said
Mr Sykes on the other end.
"Don't just wait around.
Make it happen. Children.
The Mayor. Cold emergency
beans. Tears. *That's what
I call a story!*"

Carl waved goodbye to Max and Molly
and walked away with the praise of his
boss singing in his ear. He wasn't going
to be sacked after all.

Max and Molly were left alone with Mum. She didn't look very pleased.

"I don't care what the Mayor says," she told them. "I'm not having the neighbours thinking..."

And then she stopped.

All the doors in the street had opened and the very neighbours she was talking about were coming towards them.

"We heard on the radio that Max and Molly got the street cleared," said Mrs Meadows. "We're so grateful!"

"I thought we'd be snowed in for weeks,"

said Jeremy, who was still a little blue around the edges. "But now they'll be able to reconnect the internet and I won't miss my project deadline."

"You must be so proud," said Mrs McTavish. "I hope you won't mind if I give the children this bag of my SPECIAL toffees?"

Mum didn't know what to do. Nobody in the street ever said anything nice about Max and Molly. She usually had to say sorry on their behalf.

"Well, I don't know about that," she said.

"They are real heroes!" insisted everyone.

Mum couldn't resist. "I suppose they are," she said. "I'm quite proud of them actually."

"You'll be getting them something special for their tea now, I suppose," said Mrs Meadows. "No more emergency **beans**!"

Everyone smiled.

"Of course I am," said Mum, bristling a little. "I'm just going to get the car keys and them I'm off to the supermarket to buy **pizza**."

And she walked back to the house,

leaving Max and Molly smiling sweetly at
the admiring neighbours.

"**Pizza**," said Max.

"**Pizza**..." said Molly.

SWEET AND SOUR

Later that evening, Max and Molly were each munching their third slice of **pizza**.

"You know, Molly," said Max, "I think guinea pigs might be better at ice skating than ski jumping."

"Really?" said Molly. "That's brilliant. Because I think the bird bath has frozen over outside."

"We could—"

They were interrupted by a knock at the door.

Dad went to open it. He was still wearing his head torch in case of an unexpected POWER CUT.

Standing there were Benedict, Imogen and Mrs Goodley.

"Good evening," said Dad.

"Hi, Benedict," said Max.

"Hi, Imogen," said Molly.

"They won't answer," Mrs Goodley said to Dad. "Do you want to know why? Because your children gave them Mrs McTavish's homemade super extra-thick Highland toffee. My children are not allowed toffee. And now they've eaten so much of it that their teeth are stuck together!"

"It's very nice toffee though," said Molly.

Mouths closed, Benedict and Imogen nodded in agreement.

Mrs Goodley was not as convinced.

"**Nice?**" she shouted. "It won't be nice when their teeth fall out, will it? Or when they are at the dentists having all their cavities filled?"

"Did you know that the sabre-toothed tiger had razor-sharp teeth over fifty centimetres long?" asked Max.

"Imagine the trouble they had eating **toffee**," said Molly.

This did not seem to make Mrs Goodley feel any better.

"Mr Goodley would have accompanied me to complain," she informed Dad, "but he is too upset by the direction Imogen's POEMS have been taking. They show a total lack of awe for *the wonder of the natural world* and a far more pressing concern with having **beans** for tea. I'd find out who really wrote them if my children could talk, but I've already got a very good idea! GOODNIGHT."

Dad closed the door.

"Max? Molly? What have you been up to?"

Max and Molly quickly grabbed a last slice of **pizza**. The tone of Dad's voice told them that very soon someone would be taking it away again...

The end.

HOW TO MAKE
EMERGENCY PIZZA
(EVEN WHEN YOU'RE SNOWED IN!)

You will need:
- 4 small pita breads
- 1 small jar of tomato pasta sauce
- 100g of your favourite cheese. Try cheddar, mozarella or feta!
- A selection of your other favourite toppings. Try mushrooms, onions, sweetcorn or peppers – go wild! (But NO guinea pigs. Don't go that wild.)

Before you start, tell an adult what you're planning to do. Preferably use an Italian accent and lots of hand gestures. This makes the pizza more authentic.

1. Ask an adult to help you preheat your oven to 200°C/400°F/Gas Mark 6.

2. Place your pita breads on a baking tray and spread a tablespoon of tomato sauce on each one.

3. Sprinkle each one with your cheese, either grated or crumbled and then arrange the other toppings on top.

4. Cook the pita pizzas for 15-20 minutes, or until golden and cooked.

5. Eat! Mamma Mia!

HOW TO MAKE
ABOMINABLE
ICE LOLLIES
(YUMMIER THAN A SNOWMAN!)

You will need:

- 8 ice lolly moulds (but not 8 mouldy lollies. This would be a serious mistake.)
- 250ml apple juice
- 250ml tropical fruit juice

Making these double-flavour ice lollies couldn't be simpler! To make them extra yummy, why not try adding fresh fruit like blueberries or blackcurrants to your lolly moulds as well?

1. Pour the apple juice into the lolly moulds so that it half fills each one.

2. Freeze for an hour, or until just starting to set.

3. Top up the lolly moulds with the tropical juice and place back in the freezer until solid.

5. Eat your abominably delicious ice lollies!

HANNAH SHAW is precisely five foot five inches tall and was born some time in the 1980s. She is the brilliant author and illustrator of a number of picture books, as well an illustrator for young fiction. When she isn't drawing, writing or eating (far too many) chocolate biscuits, Hannah enjoys dog agility, dancing and making robot costumes.

DOMINIC BARKER is not sure how tall he is any more as his doctor tells him

he is shrinking. He has a recurring nightmare in which he is attacked by extremely agile dogs dressed as robots doing the conga. They hit him with chocolate biscuits. Dominic has a good idea who to blame for this...